To All My Ancestors,
Known & Unknown

Natroy Publishing Co.
NY, NY

Original Copyright ©2002
Library of Congress

First Edition
Printed in the United States

978-0-9755246-2-6

JOURNEY THROUGH A ZIGZAGGED FOREST IN A DARK FACED ~~WOMAN~~ GIRL VOL. 1

- *Two Stories*

The stories in JOURNEY THROUGH A ZIGZAGGED FOREST may challenge ideals, views and opinions as literature often does. Characters, situations and storylines do not necessarily reflect the views of the author.

Ife-Gail F. Young is also author of:

- 'Journey Through A Zigzagged Forest - In A Dark Faced Girl'
  Vol. 2 *(Collection of Stories)*

- 'My Buddy' A Commemoration For Buddy Bolden, The First Man Of Jazz – *(A Novel)*

- 'Bina And The Beanpole, An Afrocentric Children's Series and Coming of Age Reader, Vols. 1 & 2' *(Chapter Books)*

- 'Mama Rue' A Celebratory And Empowerment Experience – This is a book with 18 color illustrations that promotes literacy and community.

She is also the author of many other works in various genres...all soon to be released.

Coming Next: 'After All Is Said And Done,' (A Novel)

I JOURNEY THROUGH A ZIGZAGGED FOREST IN A DARK FACED ~~WOMAN~~ GIRL
VOL. 1

Ife-Gail F. Young

Natroy Publishing Co.

CONTENTS

*This book is dedicated to the dark faced
journeys in the forest of life*

*Also for my parents, my family,
relatives and friends –
Especially those who have learned to use their
machetes well*

*Journey Through A Zigzagged Forest In A Dark Faced Girl,
Vol. 1, contains two stories, 'A Requiem For Sonnyboy,' and
'Murphy Ain't Never Lied.' Both stories shed light on social and
political strata as they address certain conditions in black
culture.*

Life is a forest – overgrown, scant, dangerous,
poignant, straight, zigzagged and oh, so beautiful.

-AUTHOR'S NOTES –

PREPARING FOR THE FOREST

The forest has waterfalls but you can miss them if you are too busy looking for traps and the small minute things that buzz around or swing on the branches or on the ground. Before you enter the forest make a checklist. <u>Machete</u>: Check. Needed to clear a path that had not been cleared before you and to slay all the fears. <u>Rope</u>: Check. To tie up the average, the normal, the traditional thing and the people with lies and deceit that stand in the middle of the clearance. <u>Box cutter</u>: Check. Needed to slash open the boxes that close their lids tightly on minds and also to remove the truth that is hard to get at without the proper tools. <u>Food</u>: Check. To nurture the brain's muscles that can sprout wings and fly above the lower levels of thought. <u>Bottle of Tears</u>: Check. To relieve thyself if the maze of the forest ever leads to frustration. <u>Laughter</u>: Check. To have a good laugh at yourself when you fall apart at the seams. <u>Sneakers</u>: Check. When the lion blocks the entrance and you must keep the journey moving despite the teeth and claws. <u>Keys</u>: Check. To unlock the door that only you can open and the space that only you can color. <u>Truth</u>: Check. To reveal that what you are looking for has always been within.
<u>Dance</u>: Check. To celebrate when you discover the journey in the zigzagged forest was just your soul's scenic route home.

WHY JOURNEY THROUGH A DARK FACED GIRL AND NOT A WOMAN?

Because the forest is beautiful in the eyes of a child who never lets the images of slums and absent meals and lack of pocket change replace her patty cakes and double Dutch and scooters and daydreams. The child if even stricken with polio and palsy is able to pick out the smallest, most beautiful thing and rave over its admirable qualities. But the woman pouts about the smallest matters until she invites the madness. And although the child learns the warnings in old folks hums and stays

1

*outdoors when grown folks bunions swell, their world is not tainted.
The red cellophane from the empty box of chocolates she found, though
she had never tasted the treats inside, has been made enchanting enough
to show life's journey still worthwhile.*
Oh, to be a girl!

*But the woman cries when the box of chocolates do not come and scorns
the beautiful red wrapping and settles for neither. She then chooses
torment, rejection and disappointment. The woman then finds hatred for
men when the child knows hatred is the quickest way to destroy the body
and soul so she looks through the cellophane and sees the rosy colors and
all promising things that the woman's eyes missed because the woman's
tears have clouded her own vision and yesterday's memories keeps
showing her how she stumbled on the dance floor again and again.*
*A child's spanking comes and goes without judgment and bitterness,
even as she chooses her own switch from the forest bush.*
*After the lashes she skips off to the candy store to satisfy her sweet tooth
for life.*
*When a woman receives a lash she falls to the ground and cries for years
and when she is sliced by the tip of the knife she cannot move for a very
long time. But when the machete slices into the child's heart she can
show you how to act as if it never happened. And that is why there is no
room in the forest for the woman who never seems to be satisfied; who
falls jealous of the neighbor who is pretty, smart and talented. So the
woman is always striking out and competing and bringing gossip and
lies and rumors and scheming to defame and set dark-faced girls up to
be scorned and always seeking to bring people down. But the pure at
heart knows the truth - that the woman longs to be a girl but cannot
leave her helm long enough to go along with the flow.*
*And for those reasons the woman is always struggling to rescue herself
from herself. She thinks fame and approval is the answer that would
make her matter.*
But women will never matter in the journey of the forest.
*Girls matter, as they write poems about the moonlight ripples appearing
like feathery quicksilver strewn across teal blue waters. There, the
haunting voices of creation wraps their harmonies around the girl's
essence and gifts her immensely.*
Oh, to be a girl!

A girl is a wondrous thing in her yellowing ribbons and sashes saved by grandmother's loyalty. Women fall and scream and break their ankles in adventures in the zigzagged forest just like in movies and she cries because the path won't run straight. The girl demonstrates agility and shrewd cunningness with scar covered knees and iodine and bandages and pedal pushers yelling 'on guard' and successfully slays the ogre with her machete in the forest den then runs happily into the maze of things and makes a game of all the dead ends the woman's mind buckles under.

Girls walk briskly for days barefoot in the forest and pebbles do not leave damage because they catch them between their toes and squeeze them into diamonds. Girls see the 'No U Turn signs and have no desire to turn back anyway. Women live in the years behind them and waste the years in front of them. And those crazy girls, they can see forks in the road and take no time trying to figure out which road to take because they know all roads will lead to a rainbow in time. Girls see 'stop signs' and crawl under them. They see 'proceed with caution signs and climb over them and when they crash they land on their fairytales and hug a happily ever after ending.
Oh, to be a girl!
Girls come to rest stops and sing jazz and pop fingers and dance and tell stories they remember from the forest flowers. Girls can be pricked by the thorns of roses and do not cry out but instead find good purpose for the bubbling crimson, like pressing pricked fingers to a friend's as to become blood sisters, or like squeezing and dripping the crimson into the mud to have red velvet mud cakes to feed their dollies, or smoothing it on their lips to wear the color that mother forbid be taken from her makeup case. Mmmwuah!
Girls leave crimson lipstick prints when they run into brick walls.
Girls are strong like that.
Oh, to be a girl!

Girls remember that stealing from others is an indication of lack consciousness or a hopeless feeling; so they give away their last crayon in the box because they know their gifts are unlimited. Girls sense the evil and ulterior motives inside people like all children can. Women often house those things that girls sense although they strive to camouflage it with their bibles and gospel and fake prayers- but girls recognize it like the stench of rotted meat.

By Ife-Gail F. Young

Women sit with their friends at corner taverns and share sad stories and the tissue box. They tear down other people's progress and are not happy until they are in control of other's lives, yet, are unable to live their own.
Girls say to hell with control and that makes them natural leaders.
Girls come together to explore every inch of the forest with sling shots and pea shooters and they leave the house prepared. Girls are clever like that. And if she is lucky and is a true girl at heart she will never become a woman and everything will always be interesting and anew.
And when the mountains appear, women carry too much baggage to pull themselves over and they slide back down to their garbage worlds. But girls climb mountains like goats and wave their conquering spirits like banners high. They cross to the other side and a new beginning.

Women are rigid and scold often, are confused, hold onto pain from choosing wrong lovers and doors and they grow tired and weary and sleep often and talk about their ships coming in and what they would do if they only had what they don't have... Girls have never lacked riches though their pockets omit a jingle. Life is their treasure of wealth even though they have had to escape the eye of the storm once or twice. But as the eye of the storm creates wind currents, girls put them to good use and let them cool the perspiration under their armpits. Then they sip on lemonade they made from the lemons the storm tossed their way.
Oh, to be a girl!
While women never have enough light to fill a room, girls give off a luminous glow always in spite of the socks with holes and the carbohydrates dinner and the tattered Sunday clothing. Women's faces look like 'worry' too soon and they allow themselves to grow unfit from sipping on self-made burdens. But girls retain muscle tone from the forest's parcourse. Women close the book and complain about what has never been. Girls say 'maybe you should read the next chapter'.
Then they swoosh ahead and stop at a tree circled by mushrooms and find flowers and bamboo leaves to make crowns for their heads. Behold! The Queen Girl! Afterwards she choreographs her day to music the wind blows her way.
Girls dance under the stars and catch lightning bugs as signs for miracles. They know they are ever there to see the good of things though they may grow old and the rainbow may disappear and the bad might become their lover. But for the moment they watch the flesh eating flowers and if they are nibbled upon they stay anew as they find ways to

camouflage themselves the next time 'round. They make maps and scribble in dirt with twigs and erase them right before the enemy scopes their plans.

Women forget how to be clever like that and the forest swallows them up whole. Then they sit like dust and wine and age and moan and weep or cheat or lie and ask their Gods over and over for forgiveness.

Girls are automatically forgiven for their transgressions because they are almost always the reactions from someone defecating on their trails. Even as girls conduct research and write scholarly books they shine like youth because...Girls live life. Girls give life. Girls claim life, Girls give love. And when the forest swallows the girl six feet under, she will fertilize a lone colorful lily that can be seen only by other grown children and will help guide them on their paths.

Oh, to be a girl!

And when the woman remembers the girl within her once made the journey easy and can be that child again, the forest will bow down and let her through and the zigzag will please her temple and she will learn that 'GIRL' is the mindset that takes

her into heaven.

As for the dark-faced boy? Tell ya a secret?

Little boys have the most fun.

But that is why my journey in a dark faced girl will continue on in this land that didn't prepare for the freedom of my soul and

yet, I have slipped out of the chains.

"Oh, you didn't know girls were escape artists too? Well just watch how this girl can escape out of the quicksand, rise like yeast and bake herself up another great adventure.

By Ife-Gail F. Young

In the forest, there are thorns . . .

She wrote on a blank page, 'A Requiem for Sonnyboy'—
"If I could, I'd kiss you in yo' blue black lips and pray you got enough love to spit back on me."

A Requiem For Sonnyboy

"If I was you I would cover my hands up every time I leave outta the house. Don't you care what people say?"

"Nope. People got nothing to do with my life," Kora returned sharply.

Aunt Ruby had been lightly disturbed over Kora's fingernails for years but Kora had been too swept over life to give them a second thought. But she had overdone it that time and chewed her nails until her fingertips bled. That meant the family would have to be on alert, for Kora's nail bleeding was always a sign of things to come. It meant her nervous energy would soon take on a dangerous form of release. It wasn't a good thing for the family when Kora had nervous energy and she had already started darting up the stairs, two at a time.

Kora was tall and slim and the color of very light brown wrapping paper. Her face was narrow and had been afflicted with a type of eczema for years; little fine bumps brought on by poor eating habits. The food had been available but her hyper nature seldom allowed her to take time out for balanced meals.

And perhaps that is why gravity had had such a love affair with her face, clinging to it, dragging it down as low as it could. So Kora looked old at forty-two. Perhaps as old as Aunt Ruby who was either sixty-two or sixty-three. Few people knew for sure. Aunt Ruby lied about things like age.

Kora announced her plans to marry abruptly. Nobody had even known she had been dating. True, she had left out each day to take pottery classes, then stayed out all night long. But even when she called home to say she'd be sleeping over a friend's house, *Helen's;* no one suspected a 'husband to be.' Boyfriend? Maybe. But suddenly Aunt Ruby wound up at the table with Kora, flipping hundreds of magazine pages, looking for a unique wedding gown.

"I just don't know what kinda man this Wali is." Aunt Ruby blurted. "What? He think he too good to meet your family?"

"Aunt Ruby, you know Mama Pearl's gonna just put him down for being an artist. She only likes men that works in factories," Kora defended.

"Nothing wrong with marrying a good provider now."

"Well, I like him just the way he is."

"Like? Womens in my day loved the man they married."

"I do love him."

"You said *like.* Which one is it? An where'd you meet this so-called man? An' do you really know him?"

"Course I know him. And he's good looking. You'll see. He looks just like a young Harry Bellefonte."

Aunt Ruby had been married before and understood both desire and practicality. Kora had been thinking of desire.

"You too old to be stuck on looks, Kora. Be different if you was twenty years old or he had Bellefonte's money."

"Me and Wali got love. We don't need money."

"Well yawl would be the first couple I know that didn't need money. But you don't have to listen to me. Be hardheaded. Time will tell everything. It's too bad people have to learn the hard way. Time is surely gonna tell it."

"That's right. Now did you ask Mrs. Murch about Sonnyboy? I sure wish I could invite him. Remember how he locked his garage and started that fire? Just like he was trying to burn himself up, wasn't it?"

"There you go with Sonnyboy again," Aunt Ruby wailed. You better try to keep your mind in the present like Dr. Rhuel said or your husband to be is gonna see another side to you. Then you might not have a wedding at all.

Aunt Ruby had been referring to those times when Kora had not been able to distinguish between reality and dreams.

After a few more tedious weeks of planning, Kora did have a wedding. Her circle of friends and relatives was small. But in all, her father had spent about eight thousand dollars to give her away including the five thousand dollars he spent on furniture and other gifts. But one thing for sure, the groom really did favor young Bellefonte and sometimes he talked out of the side of his mouth like he was tough or cool or maybe even both. He distinctively cocked his hats to the side

The couple didn't bother to move. They stayed right in the house with the rest of the family. Their plans were to save their money and move to a progressive city the following year. Somewhere artsy. The husband sold African clothing and wooden carvings and made out surprisingly well. Yet, he was always distrustful of the family and standoffish. Still, he was very good around the house. He trimmed the hedges, cut the grass and made all the minor repairs that the family had always paid a fortune to have done. After chores, he and Kora would visit the neighborhood restaurants and bars with their friends. Kora jotted poems on napkins and notepads while he'd have his hair pulled back into a wooly ponytail stressing philosophical statements to friends like, "we're artists, we're different."

But Kora truly was different. She was exceptionally intelligent. Yet, her intelligence, three psychologists said, was not to her advantage. She was known to use it in the same regard as many other geniuses used theirs...dangerously, arrogantly.

Kora grew restless in less than three months of marriage. She screamed that she needed change and that she was not able to wait until the following year to move, so she and the husband split to Chicago that first year but not before sending the family through pure, unadulterated hell. They fussed and fought twenty-four seven and Kora refused to do any housework at all because Aunt Ruby accused her of being lazy. She would show Aunt Ruby. And she also took to breaking ashtrays and kicking over chairs, the good ones with reinforced dowels.

The family was ecstatic when the couple waved goodbye in their old red van. Peace at last.

But new occupants slipped under the roof almost as soon as Kora and Wali had left. Honest bones. Children.

Aunt Ruby took them in while her niece, Tanisha, and nephew in-law, Tim, finished college. She just couldn't imagine another year of Tim rising at 5:00a.m. to work ten hours a day dipping hubcaps into a vat of molten chrome and Tanisha, working in a light bulb factory. Those things had been of her generation. So she set the young parents down and gave them a good talking to and a few months later they were on their way to campus life.

The three children hadn't been too much of an annoyance at the start, but as they grew more comfortable in the home, they began to behave like normal children. Noisily. Mama Pearl and Uncle Buse often stripped the leaves from thin green shoots to sting the children's legs but Aunt Ruby appeared like a guardian angel every time.

"Leave em lone. They got a right to be chil'ren. 'Grown folks ought not to pick on chil'ren so. They've got a right to be run and play. We was children once too. " Once she mistakenly said, "ya'll make em feel like po' Sonnyboy."

When her voice quivered out, 'Sonnyboy' she cringed over, sick to her stomach. She rushed to the bathroom that echoed a dry heaving which lasted for three minutes or more. Uncle Buse and Mama Pearl didn't bother to see about her. They knew what the mention of Sonnyboy could do.

Mama Pearl began passing out whenever she reached the top of the stairs. She was 'low sick' by the time the clinic checked her out. The diagnosis wasn't good. The doctor hadn't told her but she just knew. So she started knitting and crocheting every chance she could to fill in the solemn hours before the last one. She prayed that Kora would return, but she didn't dare ask for her. Yet, wouldn't you know it? Kora showed up early one Saturday morning. Unexpectedly. She had with her two balled up pairs of jeans, several pairs of dirty panties, a pair of dirty blue socks, a bar of soap, an opened box of tampons, a toothbrush and a half eaten Hershey's Bar. Kora's marriage had been a waste. It was senseless and unyielding. Had absolutely no direction for the entire nine months she'd been a wife. Aunt Ruby greeted her at the door.

"Well, well. Look who's back. So what happened to all them pretty clothes and furniture your father bought ya?"

"Why you asking about the stuff Daddy bought for me? Did you pay for it?"

"It's gone ain't it?" Aunt Ruby said disgustedly. "That's plain wasteful, Kora. Jest wasteful. You back to stay or what?"

"It depends on how many paintings Wali's gonna sell."

"Well you back to stay then cause that man need a miracle to sell that stuff. It wouldn't hurt him to go back to art school. Everything he paints look squished together."

"Wali paints abstract, Aunt Ruby. That's something you can't never understand cause you got a little bitty symmetrical brain like everyone else we run into. We almost starved to death trying to make a lil' money."

"Oh you did, huh? Didn't you tell me that yawl didn't need no money?" Kora ignored Aunt Ruby and started right in on the children.

"What the hell's going on? Why you got all Tanisha's kids here? Hey you! Sit down!" she yelled at a little boy. "Aunt Ruby, can't you make them sit their little asses down?"

Kora entered the house and resumed her old lifestyle as though she had never left. She resented the children getting so much of Aunt Ruby's attention and she expressed her resentments by aggravating them. Aunt Ruby would holler out, "My God, Kora you know damn well you're too old for that!" Sometimes she would add, "Why don't you go on and take a walk. The sun's mighty kind today."

Kora would snap back, "If it's so kind, then why don't you walk in it? Once she yelled, "This is my house anyway and I can make everybody move if I want to. All I have to do is call 911 and show them my deed."

Aunt Ruby never took it to heart whenever Kora had become smart mouthed like that. She knew they possessed a quasi-like need for one another, something embarrassing to each in a sense; like a prince that is caught weeping.

Mama Pearl was rushed to the hospital early one morning. Her breathing had been labored. The doctor shook his head over her chart and sent her home to be with family. Those last days would have been sweet too, had it not been for pain, that careless victor, that made her twist and groan, even with the morphine. With her room door wide open, the old matriarch's sounds of trauma were too much for the family to endure and so someone always managed to pull the door closed; softly of course, without being seen. Her strained voice, wrapped in its frailty had often called out, "who's there? Cora? Sonnyboy? That you Ruby? Who is that?" It probably had been Aunt Ruby but she wouldn't answer.

Sometimes Mama Pearl would awaken and call for Sonnyboy as if that had been a normal thing to do.

"He's not here, Mama," Aunt Ruby would tell her softly

"Where 'bout he be, Ruby? He hiding out there? Tell him I won't hurt him. Tell em he can come back now. Nobody's gonna hurt you, Sonnyboy." But Sonnyboy never appeared.

When Mama Pearl could no longer conduct her bathroom business alone, she was embarrassed but when they wrapped a diaper around her, the embarrassment became defeat and she thought of babies all the time. Sweet babies in diapers when she was awake or sleeping. Babies everywhere. As redundant as they had become, babies, they would not leave her thoughts.

It was no wonder then that she succumbed to death's call, inviting it to sit upon the corner of her bed to smooth her strained face into that of peaceful release. So she did not resemble herself in the coffin. And because she looked ten years younger, the family slept well, knowing she'd met death willingly.

But Kora did not get along well after the funeral. Aunt Ruby hadn't wanted her to go because she knew Kora better than she had known herself. There was bound to be repercussions of some kind and so she did her very best to troubleshoot the trouble before it took hold.

"Kora, wouldn't you like to stay home and help the church womens cook?" Aunt Ruby slyly suggested. "You make good potato salad. Everyone says so."

"You're just trying to make me stay home, Aunt Ruby. You think I'm weak in the mind and crazy. Don't you? Admit it." Aunt Ruby was too smart to answer.

"I'm gonna show everyone I got a strong mind. I can take anything and I'm going to my grandmother's funeral!" And she did.

The interment is what did it. When two cousins covered the coffin with the afghan Mama Pearl had crocheted for that very occasion and friends and relatives had laid flowers upon it, Kora had a terrible fit. Right in front of everyone, her entire body jerked and twisted. She screamed to the top of her lungs and clung to the coffin until people had to pull her loose. She drooled and chewed on her handkerchief and muttered, "not her," over and over again until they left the cemetery.

The funeral triggered the eruption of her long term illness. Her delicate condition that even the husband hadn't known about. She began to entertain strangers as she had done several times before. Those strangers, again, like before, were not really there. But a short trip to the hospital would cure that frenzy. And so Kora rested once again at Stellarton House, Ward Six, to straighten out the unstableness of her mind.

Kora had not always had 'that delicate condition' but she first became unstable after her mother and father divorced. It crushed her. She was only thirteen and could not handle it. Her mother died a few months later and Kora seemed to die with her. Kora's father grieved so pitifully when Kora was placed in a sanitarium that he quickly remarried for comfort. But Kora did not take to the new stepmother when she was released and hardly ever spoke to her. When she did speak, she boasted about her real mother and slung dirty filthy words at the woman. Her father moved his new wife away after Kora had punched the woman in the face and pulled out fistfuls of her hair. He signed the house over to Kora but left Kora on his sister, Aunt Ruby, and his mother, Mama Pearl. His new home became Detroit, Michigan, a place far enough away to avoid his daughter's declaration of war. He called and popped up often enough but Kora never stayed with him again, except for short visits; a half a day, an hour, or even less if Kora had forgotten to take her medication. The rest of the family caught hell raising her; not omitting Uncle Buse who stuck mainly to himself. The aggravation Kora dished out to the family only stopped in spurts. And now she was grown and again in a delicate condition. More hell to follow. Predictably.

And if Aunt Ruby hadn't been grieving so hard over Mama Pearl's death, she may have left Kora in Stellarton House a little longer but she needed someone to talk to. Uncle Buse spent his spare time in his room and the children didn't give her any feedback. So she signed Kora out after only a month in spite of Dr. Rhuel's advice not to do so. But Kora vowed she would do better around the house and she did for a little while. She assisted Aunt Ruby in the kitchen practically that entire first week.

After she'd been home a little over a month, right when she had been kneading dough, she suddenly screamed out and clasped her hands over her ears. "Oh, I'm so tired of thinking about ol' black Sonnyboy. Why I can't get him off my mind? Ooooh, he was so black, wasn't he? What do you think happened to him, Aunt Ruby? I been wondering about him for days now."

"I don't know what happened to him and why alla sudden you thinking about him again?"

I don't know why. Something just keeps tellin' me to."

"Well, maybe you outta tell that something that keeps telling you to, to tell you not to. Didn't that same something tell you to sit right in the middle of the bridge that night? Ain't that how you wound up back in the hospital?"

Aunt Ruby had won that round but Kora had not stopped wondering about Sonnyboy.

"You think he talks to his mother at all?"

"Well she said he hadn't."

"I bet he calls her house and hangs up, don't you?"

"Honey, you're too old to be thinkin' so...so much like that.

Do me a favor and sift that bag of flour."

Kora rose lazily and began sifting the flour still thinking about Sonnyboy, where he might be.

"Are there any woods around this area that he might have wandered into? Was it wild animals still roaming around here anywhere when we was kids?"

"Why you worry yourself with things like that, Kora? I know that boy ain't thinking 'bout you, wherever he is. If he ain't dead," Aunt Ruby added.

"How you know he ain't thinking about me? How?"

Aunt Ruby stopped what she had been doing and studied the troubled niece that always managed to set herself back. "We don't need you back in the hospital. The Medicaid people is already tryin' to take this house."

"They can't take my house."

"I wouldn't put it past them. You know how the gov'ment is and the doctors might think it would be best."

"I wish those quacks would tell them people to take my house. You too scared of white folks, Aunt Ruby. You should of told em to go to hell and kiss yo' you know what. I would of told em." She sank into a brittle silence for a few moments.

"Speaking of doctors," Aunt Ruby began. "Dr. Rhuel said yo' biggest problem is that you think too much. So please stop thinking about Sonnyboy."

"Somebody ought to, Aunt Ruby. I bet he got a family somewhere. I think he might be a carpenter or maybe a doctor. Remember how long his fingers was? I bet he could have been a good piano player," Kora continued.

Aunt Ruby went back to her cooking but Kora could not let Sonnyboy go that easily.

"Mama Pearl never liked him. She said he was too black to love. Now how was she gonna call somebody black as dark as she was? I bet that's why he came to haunt her in her bedroom before she died. What if it was him that choked her to death with those long black fingers? Mama Pearl said black was the ugliest color in the spectrum. She said God made it by mistake and..."

"Chile__please! God hisself came from blackness. Stepped right out." Aunt Ruby corrected. "Lissen, I can't take this Sonnyboy talk today. Not today. Where's your friend, Helen? Don't you two go places anymore? You got money for the movies?" Kora ignored the suggestion. But Aunt Ruby had grown nervous. She always did whenever anyone would talk too much about Sonnyboy. She said the "child just grieved her heart so."

Aunt Ruby whirled her big brown figure around, opened and slammed the refrigerator and cabinet doors, opened and closed the oven and filled the kitchen air with her opinions. She half talked to Kora and half talked to herself. Kora sat and scraped the deep black cigarette burns off the table with a knife and filled the air with thoughts like *"What it would feel like to be a ladybug in a carriage drawn by six black ants."*

It had been especially hot and sticky in Cleveland that night. Kora thought she would rather be anyplace else but there. The weather had somehow defined the essence of many people on her block. Hopelessness. Suffocation even. She cleared her throat that felt as if it were trying to close. Again, suffocation.

She rose and peered out of the window. A lot of people just sat on their porches and wiped perspiration from their faces and sipped beer from tall glasses. A few sprinkled their lawns and some just stared into the air. Huge Toto, was even fatter. Retired and round, he sat on his porch, legs bent and spread, his belly hanging over his pajama's elastic waistband; pajamas that he removed only when his daughter demanded he put them in the wash. He nodded on and off like a newborn and sent neighborhood children to the store for candy bars that had rotted his teeth away. He was once a handsome man, playing the field but one woman stole his heart so completely that when she left, she took every bit of his life with her.

Even Mrs. Sanders, who at one time would never have left her home without donning a hat and white dress gloves, thought nothing of inching her way to the corner store for chewing tobacco. She wore dirty housedresses and gummy slippers that knocked and skidded across the pavement. That had been suffocation.

But the saddest, most suffocating person on the block was Mrs. Murch, Sonnyboy's mother. She had lost her son to the word's malice when he was only one minute old. An unusually dark complexioned newborn, Mrs. Murch tried to deny that Sonnyboy was her baby. But people like her friend Juanita Kendall, slapped her face hard and shook her by the shoulders and said, "Now you look here, Edna. What color ya speck de baby to come out? Been fathered by Lonnie Murch. Ya can't get much blacker din' dat. Babies take after der daddy's side too, ya know. Now ya jest tell dem nurses ya sorry for accusing' em of switching ya baby. Tell em. Then you take that fine baby home and give him a good life."

So Lonnie Murch, Jr., who would grow up to be called Sonnyboy, lay sleeping blissfully on his mother's lap, her breast milk spilling down the side of his cheek, making his journey home from red light to red light.

Mr. Murch, almost as dark as his son, had been a truck driver. He had alternated his work schedule way before Sonnyboy was born; four weeks on the road, four weeks home.

He stayed away even longer after Sonnyboy disappeared and finally…he had not returned home for over a year. But his wife hadn't cared much because she had learned to generate fury for him without premeditation, for he had played a dirty trick upon her person. He simply had not mentioned that although he had been deep chocolate brown, that he had also been the lightest member in his immediate family. Sonnyboy, of course had been made in replication of the Murch family's d.n.a. and the results devastated his mother when he came out looking like that. *Soot black.*

Mrs. Murch never spoke about her son or husband. She just went about her business shaving off her eyebrows, and then drawing them back on, a little thin line, too high, which gave her a look of surprise. Her eyes seemed more deeply set than before and they were haunting too. Sorrowful. Her skin was still smooth and butter brown except for those light spots all over her legs, legs that had once been plump and shapely but had become thin and lacked muscle tone. She wasn't quite, 'right' people said but she needed no home assistance although she did talk to herself at times and peed in the front lawn where everyone could see. And almost after every Sunday service, she'd stop off at a bar and on her way home perform a sanctified dance in the middle of the street. Aunt Ruby said Mrs. Murch was punishing herself for how she had treated Sonnyboy, for helping to give him good reason for what he had done.

Some evenings, Mrs. Murch would stagger down the street. Aunt Ruby would whisper, "She's drunk again. That's what she get. She hounded the po' boy both day and night about the least little thing. Jest cause he was so dark. That wasn't right. You know it wasn't."

But after Mrs. Murch would stand on the porch swaying back and forth trying to put her key into the lock, Aunt Ruby would walk over to help her into the house. Then she'd come back saying, "Poor thing. What else could a mother do with her child when she been taught to hate him? She been taught. She pitiful."

Aunt Ruby was a true gem. She might have been the only person that had never judged Sonnyboy's skin. She had been overweight from childhood and she knew how it felt to be ridiculed, scorned and even despised by others. Mama Pearl on the other hand had been insensitive, especially in her later years. She thought nothing of degrading Sonnyboy. When Kora was still a child, Mama Pearl would say, "Now baby, don't ya go play with dat lil' black boy. He's evil jest like the devil. Jest plain black and evil."

But Aunt Ruby went out of her way to make Sonnyboy feel good about himself. And if she baked cookies and passed them out to the children, she made sure he had his share. She had even touched Sonnyboy; stroked his head lovingly and smiled in his face. Nobody else had ever touched him. They wouldn't.

But when Sonnyboy turned fourteen and learned to live on the edge of the world, balanced on survival's promise and one thin hope, he upped and left. It happened on a regular weekday. A few people said they saw him walk right past his school and climb onto a streetcar headed west. He was never heard from again.

The community attached posters on buildings and poles. The caption read: 'MISSING', Thursday, May 9, 1957, Lonnie Murch, Jr. 5'7", 130 pounds, 14 years old. Contact the Murch family at, etc... Then a picture of Sonnyboy followed the caption but little good did it do. The picture was so dark that it appeared to be just one black blur. Furthermore, the search party had consisted of some of the very children that had played the dangerous child apartheid game, contributing to his disappearance. Secretly, each child had hoped to be the one to discover his hard, flattened body glued onto a pile of leaves nearby but Sonnyboy had not given them that satisfaction. He became the biggest mystery on the Negro side of town.

Aunt Ruby kept one of the 'MISSING' posters and would look it over from time to time. She'd hang her head and cry and mutter things like, *"Lawd have mercy on a child in a foul and decadent world."* Sonnyboy remained a puzzle on everybody's mind for the next thirty years. *Whatever happened to Sonnyboy?*

Aunt Ruby broke down over dinner one night. She had served stewed chicken and dumplings and it made her think of Mama Pearl. "I guess Mama ain't gonna never taste dumplings again," she whimpered. Ain't no hand like yo' Mama's hand."

Uncle Buse started crying too. "Lawd, I wish Mama was here. Why she have to die, Ruby? Why? She wuzn't all that old"

Aunt Ruby left the kitchen and wandered into the dining room. She flopped heavily into a chair and dabbed her large eyes with a napkin. There still lingered in the hall the sad smell of shedding evergreen wreaths and Uncle Buse's sighs. When Aunt Ruby took out the family album, Kora started.

"Oh God! Quit it, Aunt Ruby. You jest quit it now. You want me to wind up back in the hospital?" But Aunt Ruby couldn't stop the flow of tears. "You DO want me to go back into the hospital, don't you? Aunt Ruby? Aunt Ruby?" Aunt Ruby could not answer.

"People something else in this house! I want everyone out. Tonight!" Kora snapped. Of course no one paid her any mind as she stomped her way out of the living room and headed for the staircase. Her robe dragged angrily behind, wiping each stair.

Her bedroom was stuffy. "The bedroom porch would be better," she thought. But it was just as stuffy and lifeless as the bedroom so she opened one of the stubborn windows and in came not only the air but also muted memories, for right beside the garage was the ragged crab apple tree that she had stood under when she was a child. The '33 Packard was still there too, her father's dusty dream. He had it towed home one day and swore that he could fix it like new. But his paydays came and left and the car just sat. It had needed too much engine work. A few years later he declared the car a classic and had one or two parts put on it but it never ran. Finally Kora and the neighborhood children turned the hood of the car into a buggy.

They pretended that it was a sleigh in the winter and a hay wagon in the summer. Excluding the sentimental elements of nostalgia, it had served no other purpose except to take up space in the small yard.

The more Kora thought about the car, the more crystallized her memories became, like those of Sonnyboy. She could almost see the incandescent purple-black boy making his way toward her with a spot of sunlight dancing on his forehead.

"Sonnyboy," she whispered. "You poor shit eating boy." Suddenly she wanted pen and paper to document her emerging memoirs of the boy who now glistened through the slight delves of time. In her attempt to locate a pen and paper she raced downstairs, making her way throughout the house like a hurricane. She jerked out dresser drawers and emptied them of their contents and left them just where they had landed. She searched the front closet, flinging Aunt Ruby's church hats and dream books to the floor.

The family stampeded into the dining room when she smashed the youngest boy's tricycle against the wall. It caused the good china to shatter in the cabinet and the picture of the Reverend Dr. Martin Luther King, Jr., to go crashing to the floor.

"Stop her. Stop her, Buse!" Aunt Ruby shouted. Uncle Buse grabbed Kora's arms and tried to hold them. But there is a strength that accompanies drive and people can become ten times as powerful, releasing an overflow of endorphins and the best thing one can do is stay out of their way.

"She crazy!" Lil' Ray screamed with wide eyes and a chuckle.

Kora grabbed a thick piece of the chubby boy's cheek and pinched it as hard as she could. The whole left side of his face puffed up and turned red. He ran screaming to Aunt Ruby.

21

Kora had wanted to punish him earlier for refusing to remove his skates when he came into the house. "You can't tell me what to do, ugly," he said. Then he stuck out his tongue at her and skated on and broke the heel off one of her pumps. But she had finally gotten him back. The sting would last a good while.

All three of the children jumped on Kora's back and pulled her hair, her gown, and gave her little dull punches in her thighs and stomach. But she didn't feel anything. She was on a mission. Pen and paper, that's all she had wanted. So she dragged along the children's weight without a thought. Uncle Buse found rope and attempted to tie Kora's hands but he had grown too slow to catch her. She snatched open the buffet drawer and like a diamond in the rock, there lay pen and paper. She calmed down quickly, mechanically, and the children climbed off her back and slid down her hips. She appeared confused; dumbfounded even, as to what had just transpired. She turned and ran upstairs. She could still hear Lil' Ray screaming from the top of the landing and Aunt Ruby fussing saying, "She's a goddamn fool, pinching my baby like that! I'm getting 'tirely too old fo' dis mess."

Kora shrugged her shoulders, curled her lips distastefully and shut the door softly. She sat upon the dusty porch settee with pen and paper, moonlight and Sonnyboy, and tried to remember the child, as he had been when she had insulted his very right to be.

Sonnyboy had been the kind of child that kept things. Kept secrets, kept hurt, kept little fires going on in garages, kept catching the little girls do the nasty with the little boys, kept coming around. Some would call him a hoax in time because the mindset of the 60's, being black and proud, had not yet surfaced. The self-hatred ingrained from slavery especially dripped from black people's hair, skin, noses, and lips. So Sonnyboy was not proud of his skin. And he had gone around asking in his own way for others to love it and to help make him proud of it, because he simply could not do so on his own. And because he was not into loving himself the other kids, several shades lighter than him, were able to train him to perform tricks. Like a dog.

On a hot summer's day Sonnyboy headed back home from the store, cupping a quart of buttermilk in a wrinkled paper bag. They stopped him, the neighborhood children did.

"Hey Sonnyboy!" Some child shouted, "I betcha won't eat that piece of candy with those ants crawling on it."

He turned to look into the children's eyes, misinterpreting their glow to mean, "we will accept you this day." So he blew what few ants he could off of the candy and squinted up his nose, opened his mouth and dropped the candy inside. There were laughs and boos but for Sonnyboy there was a deep soothing of his tormented spirit. He felt as though he had deserved the treat.

Then somebody said, "Hey Sonnyboy. I bet you won't eat this bird's egg."

The dusky child studied the blue speckled shell in his hand and thought it too beautiful to destroy but he had the children's attention for something more than his blackened skin, so he tossed the egg into his mouth and started munching, licking the drippings that flowed down his chin.

But the big dare came from Yellow Tommy, the lightest child on the block, who was admired not only because he was lighter than high yellow but also because his family had owned a late model television. Above all, he was well respected because his mother was white and worked at Joel's Candy Factory. Tommy always appeared with giant sized colorful pom pom or some other treat she'd bring home and practically every afternoon he'd pass out something tasty to all of the children on his block except, of course, to Sonnyboy. That day was no different. So after each child was nibbling on a baseball sized treat, Sonnyboy timidly approached Yellow Tommy.

"What? You want one too, nigger?" Tommy asked with a sneer. Sonnyboy nodded but kept his head held low. "Well you got to eat something first. Don't he yawl?" Yellow Tommy screeched. The children returned a high pitched affirmation.

"Did you hear my friends, blackie? You gotta eat something first!"

As Yellow Tommy stood looking for something dirty for Sonnyboy to eat, a pendant shaped blob of pigeon dung fell out of the crabapple tree and splattered the old Packard. Yellow Tommy stared at the dung and grinned with clenched teeth and said, "I give you a pom pom if you eat that pigeon doo doo."

Then he smiled at the kids, soliciting their endorsement of the daring proposition. He knew they all, including Kora, hated dark skinned people. They'd all been taught to.

Sonnyboy looked around, his gentleness bleeding; his perfectly rounded head tilted, perplexed. Hadn't he made pardon enough for his blackness when he ate the candy with the crawling ants and the bird's egg? Yet he had known no other ways to make apologies for his skin except to equate it with degrading things. And although his face was exquisitely beautiful and none of the other children's beauty could compare, he did not believe it to be so. He did not desire to believe it for he was deep dark in color and that could only mean hideous in the world that he was *not* living in.

So the children circled around him, Kora included, and pointed at the pigeon dung and shouted, "DO IT, EAT IT, DO IT, EAT IT, DO IT, EAT IT." Soon they were singing in unison. "DO IT, EAT IT, DO IT, EAT IT."

Sonnyboy quickly dipped his finger into the pigeon dung and sucked it off as though it had been a fingertip of Aunt Ruby's pound cake batter. The children all said, uggghh." Then the boys punched him in the shoulder hatefully and called him "a nasty black dog." Kora circled around him and thought about kicking

24

him in his back but instead spit in his face. Sonnyboy stood dazed with a 'damned if you do, a damned if you don't expression.'

Almost instinctively, Yellow Tommy, unzipped his pants, and peed on the coconut pom pom, slapped it into the hand of the child that resembled twilight, then aimed upwards and peed in Sonnyboy's face. Sonnyboy simply let the tainted candy fall to the ground and nodded, acknowledging to his world that day what his skin had truly meant. He nodded up at the sky too as though he were also making acknowledgement to God. Without warning, dark clouds gathered above his head and the rain began to pour. 'Had God also spat in his face, he wondered? Or had that been pee?'

The children who had been taught to hate Sonnyboy had gotten away once more with their child apartheid ritual and went into Yellow Tommy's house to watch early evening cartoons. They all felt superior in some way, stretched out on Yellow Tommy's floor while the dark and blue child stood melting in the rain. The next day Sonnyboy went into his garage and locked the door and set an old sofa on fire. Aunt Ruby had been washing dishes and saw him enter the garage when she had taken a quick glance out of the kitchen window. When the thick cloud of black smoke climbed through the decayed rooftop and orange leaping spears followed, she screamed for Uncle Buse to call the fire department. She was hysterical and hurried out the back way and burst the garage door down. Literally. She found Sonnyboy perched in a corner coughing and gagging and waiting patiently for the end. She had a hard time pulling him out for he had decided he wanted 'freedom' that day.

Mrs. Murch didn't say anything when she finally came out of the house. Aunt Ruby explained to her that Sonnyboy had tried to burn himself up along with the garage but Mrs. Murch just grabbed Sonnyboy by his shirt collar and led him into the house.

She did not even turn around to thank Aunt Ruby nor speak with the firemen when they pulled into the driveway.

The next few years passed by quickly. Sonnyboy never again played with the children. He sat on the second floor porch and stared down longingly and watched how they all skipped or jumped and whistled without him. But somehow, even while he was engrossed in his own world, one of the children would manage to pierce his soul by shouting up, "Sonnyboy is a tar baby, Sonnyboy is a tar baby."

His mother bought him a dog to curb the pangs of loneliness and it became his only friend besides Aunt Ruby. He grew tall and strong and although it did not seem possible, he grew darker. On the day of his disappearance his skin was the same color as his eyebrows. *Blacker than soot.*

A yawn broke through Kora's taut lips and pulled her away from her thoughts. For some unexplained reason, right then, she begin to feel just as betrothed to Sonnyboy as she had felt to the Bellefonte look alike.

"Oh my God," she slurred.

She had a sudden awareness, a fragile one, newborn and still emerging. What she remembered was that her light colored skin had been no more accepted than Sonnyboy's. Yes, it too had drawn disgust. Like the time Santa would not lift her upon his knee as he had done the little white girl who stood in line before her at the department store and who had been dirty and had a runny nose. Then there was the time that Bobby Sowinski, a white kid at her school whispered in her ear, "niggahs eat chittlins," then smacked his lips and ran. There also was the time a white nurse only touched her with her thumb and forefinger then dipped them into a dish of antibacterial solution.

The worse case of racism she had encountered was when she and four of her colleagues, all white, had gone shopping during their lunch break. All the store employees were white and the saleswomen kept their eyes only on Kora and the white cashier processed every woman's credit card quickly except Kora's. She called to check on Kora's I.D, her credit limit and learned other information before allowing her to leave with the merchandise.

Oh how badly she longed to tell Sonnyboy that she was sorry; that she did not know his pain would also be hers. But he was gone. Disappeared. Rode off with only a bottle of coca cola, leaving the kids, the dog, the street, his parents, and all that pain right behind, prone to travel from red light to red light, just as it had been from the day he was born.

Realizing the role she played in Sonnyboy's misery made Kora melancholy. She wished she and Sonnyboy had pricked and pressed fingers together or that she had done the same thing with him that she had with Yellow Tommy in her very own garage. Sonnyboy sat on the corner of Kora's garage roof that day after picking crabapples. He peeped through a hole and saw Yellow Tommy lift her dress and pull down her panties. She screamed when she saw Sonnyboy's bright eyes glistening through the hole without a blink. She waited for Mama Pearl's belt that day but Sonnyboy had had too much character to tell a soul what he had seen.

And now she wondered how she could tell Sonnyboy that she was sorry she had spit in his face if he didn't come back home. And she had to tell him so that she could be free. The guilt prodded her heart so brutally that it took her breath and she fell to the floor. She could not bear this in her delicate state of mind.

"Life for life, life for life," she repeated over and over.

She wrote on a blank page, '*A Requiem For Sonnyboy*', but she had a hard time finding the exact words to express the deep sorrow she felt. Finally she jotted…

"If I could, I'd kiss you in yo' blue black lips and pray you got enough love to spit back on me. Here you don' swallowed yo' shit and

danced away ever so lightly with puzzles of yo' life floatin' in the wind." Then she began writing nonsensical symbols and phrases like, *'kiss my asymmetrical mind'* and *'you is a too cool synthetic fool.'* He words had made no real sense to her but neither had the world just then. When it was too painful to continue writing she left out to search for Sonnyboy because she had convinced herself that nobody else had ever really tried.

As she strolled the murky streets, she thought about the emergence of the sixties and hoped that Sonnyboy, wherever he had been at the time, had had himself a jubilee with the mindset and had grown himself an eight inch afro. She thought about Yellow Tommy too. He had spent most of his life in and out of prison. Too many times as a child, he'd used his color to have his way…but in a white world, yellow skin doesn't count.

She also thought of Fannie Hines, the woman that could drink whole bottles of liquor and still belt out the blues in clubs until the sun came up, stroll to church and have people fainting in aisles singing, *"Sinner, Run To Jesus."* She was just as dark skinned as Sonnyboy and her life was just as tragic. They called her Big Hipped Sapphire in the music world; mean, ugly and evil, but she hadn't been. Just dark skinned. She never got a recording contract because she was sure to tell anyone that tried to use her skin as a curse or a commodity to kiss her big black ass. Then she would follow up with a threat like, 'Now who don't like it?' She defied them all. Even to her deathbed. Rumor had it that she rose from her coffin in the funeral home and carried her own headstone to her grave rather than have the fingers of people touch it that despised the color black.

The further Kora walked the harder she cried. She wanted to touch Sonnyboy's face, stroke it lovingly like Aunt Ruby had done. She spoke things out loudly like, "If there's a heaven, Sonnyboy, you gonna go with all of your black face blues and your pardons for ever being born in the first place." Then she began to mutter something about communions and a Eucharist. She wandered on.

The family didn't worry too much when she hadn't returned home by midnight because she had wandered off before in her nightclothes. But after a whole album of Nina Simone and half an album of Otis Redding, Uncle Buse and his friend went to search for her. They found her around 3:00 a.m. sitting in an amber lit alcove of a rundown tenement. Her head hung so low until they worried that she was dead.

"Kora?" Uncle Buse called softly. When she said "huh?" he jumped.

"Comon now, time for you to get on back home," he said.

He was gentle with her, sympathetic. He felt terrible when he noticed the deep canal at the nape of her neck. He'd seen that before. Mama Pearl had developed one before she died.

Kora shivered, and spoke softly with her head between her knees. "I left to find Sonnyboy, Uncle Buse. Yawl didn't have to come for me. I know my way home. I wanted to tell him I was sorry I spit in his face and called him names."

"Well you didn't find him, did ya? If he ain't showed up for 30 years, how you think you gon' just up and find him? Sides he probably dead."

"Sonnyboy ain't dead! Why you and Aunt Ruby say things like that?"

"Well, where's he at if he ain't dead?"

Uncle Buse was trying not to lose patience with her but he wanted to get back home and go to bed.

"Where's he at Kora?" he asked again.

Kora raised her head slowly, proudly and smiled. "You know. You see him Uncle Buse. You see him."

Uncle Buse only shook his head and hoped that Kora would not be taking another trip to Stellarton's Ward Six.

As for Kora, she finally felt at peace for the spit she had landed in Sonnyboy's face, for the bird's egg she took pleasure in watching him chew and the pigeon dung she joyfully saw him swallow. She felt free because she had finally realized the truth, that she and all of the black children she grew up with, including Yellow Tommy, belonged to the same circle of lies as Sonnyboy. They all swung from the same hangman's noose, those as light as cream, and those as black as soot. And those who were even blacker.

Uncle Buse escorted Kora to the car, slowly and gently, lest she did something sporadic. When she entered the car she rested her head on the inside window. Her face was void of expression and she did not speak or move.

As she made her way home from red light to red light, fresh tears formed and flowed down her cheeks like soft rain on alabaster walls and mixed intimately with the *dried pigeon dung around her mouth*. They were like the tears of a hardened widow's that falls freely from an open window. Falling tenderly. Uplifting... at last. At last. Dripping... dripping... drip...

THE END

But I have been loved by Murphy...

Entwined within life's forests are those special gifts and fancies that perch in the hollows of our minds to capture or set us free. Like vapors that escape our grasp, we travel the road of life barely gripping lovers in our hands; clinging to them incessantly until one's source becomes one's castle. Yet through the encumbering journey, we touch, if only with s-t-r-e-t-c-h-i-n-g fingertips, flutters of joy. Along the way, I touched joy, sweetly; yet parted with it painfully, and still, I remember.

Murphy Ain't Never Lied

As nature bid farewell to the chill of winter, spreading a green blanket across the rumps and valleys of earth and calling awake the buds anew, I too discovered an awakening in my soul. Rebellion. It was the spring I had professed my atheism. For years I had accompanied my mother into a Pentecostal haven where I warmed mahogany pews and clanged tambourines on my hips.

"Glory! Hallelujah! Glory!"

Not only did I sing in church, but allocated at least twenty-five percent of my earnings for tithes and spent two to three afternoons conducting bible studies or rehearsing with the choir director a new song to present to my congregation on Sunday mornings. However, I began to believe that being saved and sanctified was not justification enough to escape the same ills that affected the secular world. I watched how members in our congregation were stricken unmercifully; even those who were holy rollers and had lived their lives right, like Ethel Diggs. As if all her afflictions were not enough, she suffered a fatal heart attack while praying diligently.

"It's not right!" I protested to the whole church. "Why on her knees?"

"god works in mysterious ways," they answered, trying hard to convince me that it had been for Ethel's own good.

After that incident, though, I began to think that it made no difference whether a person believed in god or not because we all would see the same end. I acknowledged that there was wisdom and gifts humans could possess as a result of being in sync with the universe but that there could simply be no higher intelligence than nature or it would have known to intervene before my neighbor's child was crushed under the weight of an automobile. We had all cried out helplessly and begged god to save her, but the child bled profusely, then died.

"What kind of god is this?" I screamed to the crowd. "You saw! Why didn't he save the baby? A little baby? And he could have! God, why not just smash the whole damn earth and be done with us? Spare our suffering!" I yelled. Then I covered the child with my scarf and wept.

From that moment on, I felt that if there was a God then he might have been sadistic and that humans were simply life stragglers trying to find a way into a mythological heaven that kept floating further away. Had an insensitive God like this really made man? Or had man made this kind of god? In any case I concluded it would be better not to believe at all. So I didn't. I begin to think that nothing was higher than 'nature' and religion was simply 'life'. "To hell with your gospel!" I once shouted to a visiting choir at my university. "There is no god!" Then Murphy came home after spending four and a half years on the east coast, and I began to wonder if just maybe___ there *was* a god.

Murphy was tall and imperially slim. His complexion, a brownish-golden hue, contrasted stunningly with stark white teeth that flashed like lightning as he spoke. His hair? long and nappy, and had fused itself into dreadlocks with sun baked ends.

I asked Murphy why he wore his hair in dreadlocks for they were not at all popular at the time and he told me that he felt oppressed wearing his hair any other way. Then he laughed at my hair, saying black people don't celebrate their own look when they straighten their hair; they celebrate the white man's look. But his locks, he said, were pleasing to Jah who had ordained he grow exactly the way he had been planted. Locks, he explained were the umbilical cords that operated like antennas, connecting one with the soul of the universe.

"You know Shay," Murphy said grabbing a fistful of his hair. "The universe called my name two or three times, but until I grew these antennas, I didn't answer. But one day I stumbled upon my light. Your light is your essence and purpose. You gotta protect that forever. Don't let anyone dim it cause it's the only thing we possess that can represent the fruits of the soul."

When Murphy was not operating a self-financed soup line, he could most often be found at a library or at the youth recreation center. The gym at the Center was the meeting place where mostly young to old boys congregated to talk, partake in sports and sometimes pull a slick street deal or two. Murphy hung around the gym to enlighten the younger fellows about things like politics, manhood and history. "You got to know where you came from, before you know where you're going, Brothas. Don't forget that," he'd tell them.

"No, no. We won't," they promised.

And wherever Murphy would walk, the boys, like baby ducklings, toddled behind, unaware that their eyes said "this man is more than wonderful."

Some boys tried to imitate Murphy and walked around with books that they hadn't even read but many were original scholars. Murphy called the wannabes "purpose-traitors."

A real messiah of E. 79th Street, he raised truth seeking youths and adults six feet off the ground with his lectures. He had been the greatest influence in young men's lives besides their first piece or Thunderbird Wine, whichever had found them first.

I often saw how young boys in our church had taken the wrong path. Nothing seemed to be able to turn them around but Murphy. He'd just talk to them and tell them where they fit in. They'd listen and straighten up and become respectable young men in the community. How had it been that Murphy could do that for them but not church? Who was Murphy really?

Once I peeped into my mother's bedroom and saw her praying. I had a strong impulse to run to her and pull her off her knees and give her back her dignity. Instead I asked, "Ma, why do you continue to believe in something that never answers your prayers? You have absolutely no proof this Jesus ever existed. We are our own saviors, Ma! Black people. We have always had to save ourselves. Where was Jesus when we were in chains for hundreds of years? Why did he let that baby die? Why are babies all over the world are dying?. Why would he let all of mankind suffer because of a sin Adam and Eve committed thousands of years ago? And how can he ask us to forgive if he didn't forgive Adam and Eve? Am I wrong to feel this way, Ma?" She ignored me. That's when I heard felt myself say, "Murphy is the closest thing to a messiah that's ever come into our neighborhood! He's worked miracles with the youth, he's turned this neighborhood into a safe place to walk at night."

Her eyes darted side to side, an old nervous habit.

"So what are you saying, Shay? You want me to pray to Murphy instead?"

Well, I hadn't said that but suddenly I envisioned hundreds of middle-aged women with issues of blood chasing after Murphy. "You know, Ma," I said. "Maybe people *should* try touching the hem of Murphy's garment for a change. They might get a healing *and* a bowl of soup."

She called me a backslider as I made my way to the porch to sit and think and admire the clouds as I often did but the factory smog had all but covered them. I hated smog for I had developed the utmost respect for nature.

I could barely maintain a shoddy efficiency on 85th street with my part-time job at the record shop when my father hit the number. Big! He gave me money and bought my mother a brand new 1981 Chevy. I drove it to the library to show it off, with hopes of running into Murphy. Almost as soon as I pulled into the lot, Murphy approached the car, but he did not *see* it.

"Sistah. Sistah Shay, can I talk to you? This is real important." He proceeded to show me his recently published book of poems. They were very powerful verses sandwiched between a brightly illustrated cover.

"Sistah, I'm asking for donations to try to move this book on out to the people. We got a job to do. I need you to jest pitch in for a good cause if you can."

"What you need, Murphy?" I asked unnecessarily. I knew that anything Murphy would have requested of me was within reason. Anything.

Unbeknown to Murphy, I had loved him from the second he had set foot on E. 79th Street. I was ten years old, he sixteen. When he was a newspaper carrier, I would rise at 6:30a.m., and in obscure daylight from a fort built with polyester, I'd peek through the partings of our living room drapes and just watch him walk from house to house as he delivered papers and that was really quite filling enough for me, because as so many the television commercials I watched had claimed about their detergents, just a little bit of Murphy too, could get the job done.

Murphy continued speaking about his mission while my eyes roamed to the V-opening in his dashiki. His chest looked hard and immortal and was covered with coils of shiny black hair. The handsomely chiseled face with full purple lips was sacrosanct and drew me in, but his deep-set eyes always saw something inside of me that I didn't even know I had. So that day I refused to make eye contact with him and looked down at his feet that were strapped in sandals. It was then that I realized Murphy was not quite as perfect as I had declared him to be. *He was missing half a toe.*

Embarrassed for Murphy, that I had discovered the one flaw to encompass his being, I searched for something else to focus upon, but my eyes couldn't get past his groin area. I, unlike Murphy, have many flaws. So, succumbing to my imperfect imagination, I wondered what it would be like to lay with Murphy.

Pimp finesse rested in Murphy's hands. Fortunately, he was on the defense, always shielding his mind from the erotic kisses of women who would disrupt the mission within his soul. Women who only sought to replace his 'light' with dark rooms, thighs, wetness, warmth, and wiggles. "Ooh, do it baby, baby," these women would say to Murphy if they could, then turn him into an ordinary man, like Yodel or someone.

"Universe," I whispered. "Spare him from that kind of spanking. Turn Murphy over to me."

"So that's what I'm talking 'bout Sistah, Shay. Shay?" He called me out of my daydream adding, "...and I know yo' head is always in the right place."

I raised my eyes from his groin area, quickly, shamefully, and was unable to determine if I had embarrassed him because he gave me one of his most dazzling smiles. I departed Murphy's company that day twenty dollars poorer but much richer in social allurement.

Within the boundaries of my shoddy efficiency, I thought of fools in love and confined myself to the truth; that I was one indeed. Just three weeks earlier I had called Mason, a big mouthed patron of Yodel's Bowling Alley, a fool because he cried on the barmaid's dust cloth when his woman threatened to leave him.

He said to the barmaid and a few of his buddies, practically shouting, "Ella! Hey yawl! Lissen hyeah! I love my woman so much, I a drink her dirtee bath water."

"Yeah? Go 'head, you fool!" Ella answered.

"An' next time come up with an original line!" a thin short woman shouted.

Alas, what goes around indeed will come around because I soon understood what poor Mason had felt. Like me, he needed help over the hump of love. Had Murphy asked me to be his footstool, I just might have considered. I loved him that much! I just did. What more can I say?

I had almost fallen asleep by daybreak when a loud foghorn disturbed the silence as was done nearly every morning. I rose mechanically and my mind returned to Murphy where it stayed all of my waking day. Murphy... Murphy... Murphy... Murph...Murphy...

Yodel's had been my hangout. Really it was just a dinky hole in the wall of a use ta be thriving bowling alley. High operating costs had closed the bowling section down a long time ago but Yodel still used the bar, leaving the bowling balls and shoes to sit hauntingly, like dusty ghosts stacked uselessly on racks .

Excessive drinking, curtsies and bows to barstools and singing on an amplified microphone had been common practices at Yodel's. It had been alright to wiggle and move seductively in the middle of the dance floor too because no one would ever 'huly guly' women from behind or touch legs, breasts or thighs that were not served over the counter with fries. But the men did sometimes serenade...excuse me...did I say serenade? Well I meant *annoy*. They gave such awful impersonations of the great Temptations members, Eddie Kendricks and David Ruffin singing 'you got a smile so bright,' and 'I've got sunshine on a cloudy day', until the women would cry out, "Okay! That's enough! I'll pay for my own damn drinks. Just shut the hell up!"

And even I flopped on the corner of the stage floor and did a poor take off of Sarah Vaughn, singing, "Lover man, oh where can you be?" Then I would act mysterious and pretend to have many lovers and laugh low and menacingly, but really I just wanted Murphy.

One particular afternoon I entered my hangout to initiate a plan where Yodel could generate some real revenue. However, I wanted to help Murphy too. He needed more money for his soup line. Well, I was disclosing the plans of a book signing to Yodel but not to the nosy barmaid who was quite old but she had a youthful and very pretty face.

"Trust me, Yodel. You can have a book signing just like the bookstores."

Ella's breathing appeared sporadic and she wobbled her head at the suggestion. Then she sucked on the hole where her two front teeth had been and said, "Fuck a book signing!"

"I'm not talking to you Ella, I'm talking to Yodel," I blurted. She ignored me and continued.

"What fool gon' come to a book signing at a mothafuckin' bar? Ain't nobody wanna hear no poetry and shit. All folks wanna do on Friday is drink!"

"And fuck," added a regular.

"That is not true," I defended. "Those are stereotypes."

"Stereo...what?" Ella shouted. "See that's what I'm talking bout! These goddamn college kids alway trying to get smart!"

She rolled her eyes at me and began tossing dirty glasses into the sink so hard until Yodel yelled, "Whoa, Ella! Baby, what the fuck you doin'?"

I knew that I would have to corner Yodel when he was alone. I watched and waited and stepped outside, then back in again and watched and waited until finally I caught him alone.

"Here's the thing, man," I began, "you and Murphy can help each other out! He can help you attract a clientele that will spend some real money in this place and you can help him sell his books."

Unconditioned to change it took almost three solid hours to convince Yodel. All the while Ella gave me the dirty eye, preferring to have a drunken atmosphere where she felt like a servant rather than a cultural atmosphere where she could feel like a 'queen'. But poor Ella had negated her own worth much of her life and this situation was no different. It scared her to think she would have to be accepted. However, I had gotten my way. Murphy would have his book signing at Yodel's.

When Ella received the news that the book signing was on, she dipped her hand into her cleavage, pulled out a joint and went on break. She stood just inside of the back door as she had always done and inhaled the smoke deeply. Marijuana affected her differently than other people I knew. She could suddenly contract an itch all over her body which might require that she peel out of her clothing. Maybe I shouldn't say this, but once I noticed Ella scratching her stomach and backside after smoking a joint. She looked miserable. Then she slipped out of he underwear, stuffed them in a drawer and continued serving her customers without draws! But nobody knew that.

And now Yodel had said 'yes'! So twirling around in great satisfaction, I headed for the back entrance which would set me on the path closest to the library. I almost stumbled over Ella who had curled up at the bottom of the doorway with the demeanor of a slinky feline in heat; malevolence stuffed inside her jaws. Her mouth and eyes were drawn down and the pretty face had turned disgustingly ugly. I looked away.

"Excuse me, Ella. Can I get by?" I said, not wanting her to know that I knew she looked terrible.

"You tryin' to change the atmosphere here, ain't ya? You sayin' Yodel's ain't good 'nough for you?" she slurred.

"Ella, recitals are what's happening ." She did not hear me.

"I knew yo daddy," she began. "He was a arrogant bastard too."

I was infuriated and wanted to attack her, scratch up the cold woman's face but the fact that she had known my father was somehow more intriguing than the anger her words had provoked.

"Did she really know him?" I wondered. "And how did she know him?"

Ella yawned and scratched her neck. "Yeah I knew that mothafucka," she said slowly with a grin. "He spent yo' milk money fo' my ass when I was on the streets."

Again, I was infuriated but couldn't get into something I really knew nothing about. The best thing I could do at that moment was disappear.

"Excuse me," I said again. "I have to leave now."

"Fuck you girl," she said slowly. "You bettah go on' out the front door."

Appearing fragile and debased, Ella managed to hike up her midsection, reach under her skirt and peel off her panty hose. She balled them up and threw them in my face. I stood immobilized.

"That's right. Fuck you and fuck Yodel," Ella whined. "That bitch git in my face again, I slash huh throat an she know it too. Here you go and give huh a reason to come here."

She had been referring to Yodel's live in girlfriend who was very literary and not particularly attracted to Yodel's bare floor, beer scented, hole-in-the-wall. But a book signing was just the event that could bring her through the doors.

"You ain't gon change things 'tween me and Yodel, girl, cause I ain't gon let you," Ella threatened. "I a slash yo throat, Yodel's and hers too! I don't give a fuck 'bout going to jail!"

For some reason those words had rung in my ears. Perhaps it was because no one had ever made a weapon of their panty hose and threw them in my face. Yet, what could pitiful, toothless Ella have done? An unfortunate younger Ella had been a prostitute and most of her threats were merely the mastery of street talk, which sounded a lot more dangerous than it actually was. Besides, she had given that life up a long time ago and cringed to think about it. Still she intimidated me, so I backed away from her cautiously, observing her butcher-knife eyes that looked so tired and sad. I had never seen anyone look so tired; so worn to the soul as Ella did that day. I decided that it *would* be safer to make my exit through the front door.

I strolled down the sidewalk quite triumphantly but was almost stampeded upon by high school girls that screamed and giggled at Old Man Payne who stood in his third floor window again, exposing his private anatomy. To make matters worse, Crazy Creighton was angrily making his way towards me. Ella's wrath had been enough for a twenty-five year old high-spirited woman, so I crossed to the other side.

Two weeks later Murphy entered Yodel's dressed like a Yoruba king. I had gotten rid of the straightened or 'oppressed hair' *(as Murphy called it)* and replaced it with a very short natural that made my face look much younger and clearer. Murphy was impressed.

"Sistah, you coming along," he said. Then he ran his fingers through my hair and pulled my head close to his chest as though he was going to kiss me; but instead just patted my cheek as a little boy would pat his puppy.

His book, *In A Complicated Place,* was displayed creatively and sat amongst fliers that announced future community events.

Ella had been dressed beautifully, unlike I had ever seen and she had all of her teeth, which was a shock to everyone. But how she suffered that evening with those two front teeth. She mispronounced all the words beginning in 's' or 't' and she pushed the teeth out with her tongue then drew them back in over and over again

People that knew and admired Murphy began to pour in. They sat eagerly, anticipating the event. Some bounced and spun around on barstools, a few sat at tables and others lounged in the bowling section. Murphy stood alone graciously receiving the sprinkle of sunlight that poured through the window. Patriarchal as a high watchtower, all-knowing, his light shone brightly, untouchable.

My parents hobbled in as though they were older than they actually were and I led them to a seat close to the microphone. I could detect nothing in my father's and Ella's eyes that gave hint that they had ever known one another or had ever seen one another for that matter.

"Black folk something else," Yodel said. His deep brown face was striking as it glowed with the freshly applied lemon scented lotion. He puffed out his chest and lit a fat cigar, something I'd never seen him do before.

"Now this different!" Yodel bragged. "This is pure-dee class. That's all I can say. Look at that shit!"

He pointed to a group of very dignified looking men and women dressed in an array of styles and colors from African to contemporary Western. They all seemed to carry briefcases or had important folders and magazines tucked under their arms. Unlike Mason, who screamed and shouted after a strong drink or two, these men and women spoke softly and laughed amongst themselves.

"An' this only the first one," Yodel stated proudly through a cloud of offensive cigar smoke.

"What you mean the first one?" Ella snapped, rolling her eyes at me. "This a bar, Yodel, not a liberry."

"Aw baby, look how much money we don' already made." Yodel grinned and hugged her, but she pulled away, unimpressed.

"I ain't thinkin' 'bout money," she cooed. "I'm thinking 'bout atmosphere. Look at how it don' changed our reglars. Dey ain't comfortable with dis bullshit."

We looked around and spotted Mason who sat erect in his suit and tie. His hands were folded on the table and he looked fearful, if anything, for the Yodel's that had occasionally demanded a loud shout or two before, suddenly required best behavior, deep thought and questions with long ambiguous answers. The regular customers, like Mason, could have chosen to stay home or could have gone to Yodel's competitors, but instead they came in satin and ties because they wanted to be there.

"Well if you gon' be having this kinda thing again," Ella threatened, "then you best to place a ad for a new barmaid!"

She quickly turned her back to Yodel and ran smack into his Number One.

A homely looking woman she was, not at all attractive. She was almost as old as Ella, but she did not have the hardness about her brow and mouth. The two women practically stared one another down while Yodel tiptoed to the other side of the room.

Murphy sampled practically every tray filled with fruits and vegetables. He grabbed my hand as I passed by and introduced me to his Jamaican friend who also wore locks that were even longer than Murphy's. He was almost as charming as Murphy too and just as tall.

"Ey Shay, love, so beeuteefula 'oman, you are," his friend said. He had a comical air about himself and I couldn't help but laugh as he bowed and kissed the back of my hand. When he wouldn't turn it loose, Murphy gently pulled me away from him. They shared a secret laugh before Murphy led him to the display table.

Then...I saw *him* out of the corner of my eye! *Crazy Creighton*. He looked sneaky and frightful as he cupped his hands to peer into the window. Needing acknowledgement of his existence, he tapped on the windowpane with his fingernail to gain attention. Nobody wanted to see. Suddenly he barged through the doors like a combat soldier. Standing at the alpha and omega of his alter ego, he stared grievously at the crowd. He was the essence of the word negative and was detrimental enough when he was sober, but that day he staggered. Although he was black like the rest of us, he felt that nothing good could ever come from black people. He despised himself and everyone else that looked like him. He didn't wear an ankh or symbolic relic like Murphy and some of the other men did. Instead, he had hate dangling around his neck and it was coupled with angst-filled eyes. To sum it up, he was a walking time bomb with intentions to explode wherever he could do the most damage.

"What's goin' on here?" he demanded of a patron and myself. We did not answer for we knew his purpose for breathing.

"Fuck yawl then!" He said, spraying us with his saliva. Then he walked away swinging his arms side to side in a gait that dared anyone to mess with him. We exhaled.

"Ay Yodel, mane__, what you got going here?" he shouted.

His face was strained and he appeared upset about the event that was about to take place without his presence. Yodel was not at all pleased to see the skinny young man who quickly put on a fake smile.

"Sit down Creighton, and don't start nothing or I'm going to ask you to leave."

"Leave? Ask me to leave for what? I just wanna know why all these jake looking mothafuckas in here?"

Ella turned, nodded and agreed with Crazy Creighton. I wanted to slap her silly for that because the slightest bit of encouragement could set him off.

"It's a recital and book signing for Murphy," I said quickly. "So please, please, jest..."

"Murphy who?" Crazy Creighton demanded. "I know you ain't talkin' bout that nappy headed mothafucka!"

"Will you stop cursing in here!" I screamed.

"You don't tell me how to talk, girl!" he screamed back.

"Where Murphy? Where that punk mothafucka at?"

He spotted Murphy and crookedly made his way over to him.

"They say you wrote a book, mane__. I 'on't believe it."

"Brother it's true, but that's not rare. Millions of people are willing vessels of creativity. I felt like I had something to say so I took my words to a printer. I'm just a drop in the bucket."

"Where the book? Where it at?" Crazy Creighton snapped. He looked around in fury and before Murphy could say another word, he animatedly staggered in long strides over to the display table, and inspected Murphy's book. He flipped the pages quickly and laughed wickedly, as if Murphy's poems were not up to par.

"Don't you try to bring him down!" I yelled. After a tough struggle I finally yanked the book from his hand.

Murphy's voice poured through the speakers. "Testing, testing 1,2,3. Would everybody please be seated? Before I start, I'd like to inform those who don't know, that I've been given a new name.   Today I am Ntomokenze Mustafa Osei." Or something like that.

Well that had been a real tongue twister for most of us, and impossible for Ella with her two front teeth. But the people softly repeated the strange name over and over, trying to ingrain it into their memories

Belligerent as always, Crazy Creighton stood up to make protest.

"Ay Murphy mane____, I been knowing you since we was kids and you gon' always be jest plain Murphy to me. Fuck that new name shit!" He tossed his head back and laughed.

Murphy answered him with grace.

"Brother, cocoons break open for butterflies. Nuff said." Everybody had to think about that for a moment.

"I wanna take this special opportunity," continued Murphy, "to thank each and every one of you for supporting me in my efforts to give the people what they need."

"Who need?" Crazy Creighton asked. "I 'on't need no book of bullshit poems! I need me some mothafuckin' money! That's what I need!"

People turned their heads with their mouths open, in complete shock. Even Mason who had began to appreciate the cultural manifesto disapproved of Crazy Creighton's outburst. A short, thick man that looked like he could put a hurting on the world's Heavyweight Boxing Champ threatened Crazy Creighton. After he sized up the man, Crazy Creighton must have decided that he did not want a fight because he grew quiet. At least for the moment.

Murphy ignored the chatter that came from the interruption and continued to express acknowledgements that included my name. Then he began the recital. People moved closer, crossed their arms and legs, tilted their heads, and gave Murphy their full attention. Crazy Creighton pretended to be laughing at Murphy's poems, but I caught moments where he was listening intently and appeared truly shocked at the depth of Murphy's mind. Even Ella strolled from behind the bar and sat closer to Murphy. Her chin tilted up then dropped downward. Embarrassment and relief sat upon her countenance. Somebody had finally understood her. And I thought I saw a tear form in the corner of her eye before she brushed it away with her fingertips.

"I know the extent of your weary pain, my lonely forgotten goddess...," Murphy continued.

Everything was going quite nicely until a gentleman cleared his throat. Crazy Creighton recognized him as the young man that had left his sister standing at the altar and he shouted clean across the room in his most intimidating voice.

"Hey Raymond! Mane___I'm kicking yo' ass!"

People looked around but remained seated as Murphy continued his recital. "...and my comely black queen, siphoned of the Nile..."

Murphy's young disciples headed toward Crazy Creighton but it was too late. Like a streamline missile he charged through the air smashing tables and heads along the way. In bobcat style, he scratched, pushed and pulled in an attempt to get at the young man who used his head wisely and quickly ran out.

Well, the time bomb had exploded and everyone was a target. The women screamed as Crazy Creighton landed blows on the faces of at least ten males, including my father. People began to push and huddle into one another, attempting to capture the bomb.

"Git yo mothafuckin' hands offa me!" he shouted. "I ain't playing! I said git em off!"

In a matter of minutes the whole club was in an uproar.

"Call the police!" somebody begged. I rushed to the phone but remembered that Murphy said black people should handle their own altercations so I ran to check on my mother instead who had overreacted to the incident. She clutched her bosom as if she were having a heart attack and called Yodel's place low lifed and begged me to leave.

Ironically, Ella, who had been against the gathering from the beginning, appeared to be the most disturbed. She whimpered and poured a triple, which she killed in two swallows. Then she cursed Crazy Creighton who was taking on at least five men at the door.

Murphy stood at the microphone and begged for order. "Sisters and brothers, please! Sisters...Sister Jenkins, Brother Creighton, Brother Al, please... Can I have everyone's attention please? Attention please!"

A large group of Murphy's associates gathered in one of the bowling lanes, bewildered and unsure of what to do while Murphy continued to plead, looking as elegant as a crescent moon and unfortunately just as effective. Finally Murphy said...and I will never forget these words as long as I live, for they were offensively effective. He said, "WILL THE REAL NIGGAHS PLEASE STAND UP!" Well of course everybody scurried to sit down except Crazy Creighton, who escaped with curled fists, declaring war on the young man.

The rest of the evening went well. The climate was recaptured and not once did Mason shout. In fact, he purchased four books from Murphy and shook his hand again and again. Ella sat perched in a chair in the corner as she read Murphy's book, too absorbed to even care about the affection Yodel was giving to his Number One.

Murphy sold fifty-two books in all and declared the event a success.

"How was it a success, Murphy?" I asked. "It was sabotaged."

Feeling ostracized, I began to clean up. My eyes filled with tears. Murphy smiled and stood before me. He took the dishes out of my hands and placed them back upon the table. Like a disguised dream shedding its facade, my face melted on Murphy's chest. His heart beat hard while the scent of Egyptian Musk stomped its way into my memory. We stood pressed together, unaware of time.

"Ummm, you feel so good up close like this," he said in a muffled tone. "Now tell me, why are you crying? Everything was perfect. Don't you know that you did something for me that no one has ever done? You have helped me fulfill my dream. I couldn't be happier than I am right now. You have to believe that." Then he wiped my tears away with the ends of his locks. "Come home with me tonight," he whispered.

I moved my lips to say 'yes' but no sound came. I had begun to hyperventilate, but he understood my answer. He backed away, staring into my face with a vulnerable silence, even as he gathered his speakers and microphones. The 'baby ducklings' helped him load the equipment in his very used van, gave him the black hand shake and saw us off. I was nervous and talkative on the way there but Murphy said not a mumbling word.

In this world are pockets stuffed with heavens that can be extracted with the right position of the fingers and finagling of the wrist. But the clumsy hands of a thief can leave heaven shattered and bleeding from its gist.

The lectures that Murphy had been so well respected for were conglomerates of the many books that were scattered across his floors and tables. Two walls were plastered with reggae stars and political leaders and wise sayings. Another wall was covered with a large red, black and green banner. A mobile that read ONE LOVE hung from the center of the ceiling above his mattress in the living room. I was not sure what the phrase meant at that time but I know too well its meaning today.

Our conversation was awkward. Murphy talked about his mission and I spoke about my classes and professors.

"Don't lose focus in that college, Shay," Murphy warned. Then he said, "Negroes kill me bragging about all their degrees but it's nothing to be proud of to have the white man's education. It was something forced on us. We would have been getting our own if we hadn't been stolen from Africa. An' I tell sisters and brothers, don't let the remnants of slavery stop you from learning as much about Africa as you can. I tell them to learn and document so our children will know the truth. If we don't set it out, who will? Half of them don't listen though. A lot of them just take up something that can make them a lot of money when they get out. And there's nothing wrong with that as long as they remember that we can always use another soup line. We shouldn't have to go to the white man to get food when we're down on our luck. He never cared about us. We forget too often that we didn't come to this country on our own will. You didn't forget, did you?"

"Now Murphy, you know I couldn't forget something like that. I'm reminded every time I step out of the house and see so many of our people homeless and without jobs."

We grew quiet after awhile, anticipating the moment. I leaned my head on his chest and he gently nibbled on my ear. Within seconds we were taken over by passion. We moved slowly toward his lumpy mattress and fell upon it. He was first to remove his clothes. I stood tensed. When he drew me near and unbuttoned my blouse, a streak of anxiety traveled from my pelvis to my stomach. I closed my blouse and turned away.

"What's wrong baby? Shay?"

Standing stark naked, he drew me close again and kissed me. I felt an urgency to clarify a few things.

"Wait! Listen Murphy, you have always been my lover, right? I, I mean I have *always* loved you and your Rasta ways from the time you were a boy; and I think of you constantly and when I hear your voice my legs get wobbly and I cannot think... I want to do this, I need to do this. I mean I'm here because you are special to me. Not because I'm easy or anything." I felt relief dampen my cheeks.

"I knew all that," he said and flashed his white lightning smile. "Aw, Baby Girl, don't cry." With his tongue he licked away my tears.

Those words, "baby girl" had made my toes curl up. They would ring in my ears forever. Just the way that he said them.

Then in a shaky voice, he said... "You are a Rasta love and I have loved you from the time I came back to town. It's your personality...and intelligence. And you are so beautiful, inside and out... almost intimidating to a man."

Our lips met again, more honestly. Afterwards I felt comfortable enough to disrobe. Murphy seemed pleased, saying, "Ah, I knew you were made like this." His mouth cupped over my nipple and his suction helplessly drew me in. I wrapped my fingers around his locks and it was then that I was met with such a strange and unexplainable force which was like a bolt of lightening so powerful that I was knocked to the floor.

"What was that? What happened?" I asked, looking for some reasonable explanation.

"You touched me, Shay. I'm sure," he said. Then he nervously turned away. "Music, let's see." He shuffled through his album collection. "Here's something you'll like".

He dimmed the lights and we lay face to face. "You scare me," he whispered. "Of all the women I've ever known, only you have been able to touch my light." My toes curled again. Then his lips brushed over and closed my eyelids, similar to that of an eclipse. When I opened them, I saw that he had given me sight. There was a heaven in the room that I had overlooked before.

As we conveyed our feelings for one another, I imagined the moon and stars were spectators that glowed brighter each time we sighed, murmured soft talk, sweet talk, nasty talk... Our bodies tangled, rose together, dropped, were hot and sticky..., we sweat and moaned. "Shay," he called out.

A thousand echoes reverberated in my soul. I felt I would explode. Through the thickets of dark fruition, I heard myself respond..., "*My God.*"

Our hands clasped together, tightened and trembled, loosened, tightened and trembled over and over until finally our bodies fell limp. Feeling anew, I realized amidst the storm of love, Murphy had taken the time to baptize me. The hull of midnight I lay cradled within a dark that was piercingly bright, for I had searched inside for my soul and instead found two of them. Murphy rested between my thighs while I thought of husbands. Finally he rolled over and we slept.

The next morning Murphy said that he would not see me again. I was shaken.

"Murphy, no! You used me!"

"I did not! I thought you were the one person that understood me! Shay, look at me! You would absorb too much of my light.

You leave me weak. What will I give to the people?"

He lifted my face to his. "Look at me! Suppress your ego. Now listen! You cannot go with me on my journey of life...it is *my* assignment." He released my chin then dropped his head sadly. Through a brittle silence, he said, "you should finish school and go down your own ordained path for now. That's all I have to say on the subject."

I continued to make argument, but after a few minutes he left the room. I rushed tearfully into the bathroom and ran a tub of hot water and sat in it with a diffused ego. With my eyes closed, I imagined ways to get even with Murphy. More than once he had likened his locks to Samson's. Well then I would liken myself to Delilah and hide scissors beneath his mattress. As soon as he would turn his head I would sever the umbilical cords he grew for his Jah. Punish him! Make him a mortal man.

When I returned to the living room, Murphy had placed our breakfast on trays. He sniffed the air.

"What is that delicious fragrance you're wearing?" he asked. "Come here. Can I taste it?"

He sniffed playfully around my neck and bosom until I began laughing. Then I backed away, my heart in my throat as I neared the door, feeling defeated but trying hard to be as spiritually mature as Murphy.

"Well, I'll see you around, Murphy."

"Wait! You're not ready to leave yet, are you?"

"Well, given the circumstances, I think it would be best."

"No. Come on. Sit down. Eat something. Oh, come on. The food is good. Try it."

He pulled me toward the bed and I sat down to eat. It was an awkward moment. I felt unwanted, as if he were humoring me. But he appeared to be in deep thought.

"What do you want out of life, Shay?"

"Happiness. That's all I want, just happiness."

"Then happiness should be a journey," he said. "Not a destination. We're both lights. Look. Let me show you something. Now what happens when I flick this switch up and down? What's taking place?"

"You're turning the light off and on."

"More than that," he said. "The light is traveling. It's only natural that light should travel."

He played his guitar for me after we had eaten. "That was a redemption song, Shay. I give Bob Marley respect every time I do one of his songs. The brother was real, ya know. He inspired a whole lot of people just in his music. You do like Reggae, don't you?"

"Sure, I like it. I don't know much about it but I guess that doesn't matter."

"What doesn't matter? Sure it does. Reggae is not ordinary music, "he stressed. Then he went on to tell me about Jah and Haile Sellassie, Reggae and all about Bob Marley's life. Later he elected to release bits and pieces of his own life.

"I never hung out with anybody. You know that yourself... although I got along with them. I was just never interested in the things most people did. But give me a heavy book, and I was okay. It was like a challenge to break down the meaning, ya know? An' politics was my thing. When I was only fourteen, my people called me 'old man'. They said I had an old soul and was wise and they wanted me to be a politician but Jah had other plans for me. Besides, I wouldn't have made a very good liar."

He laughed loudly with his head drawn back and I followed. Suddenly he stopped laughing. He sighed and rubbed his fingers through my hair and held me close as an expression of sorrow rode across his face.

"I never really had a childhood… my old soul made me too responsible. I knew what I was about by the time I had turned ten. Hey! Did you get enough to eat?"

"I won't need another meal for days."

"You sure? I've got more."

"No, I'm full, honest."

"It's good natural food. It'll give you a lot of energy to___well, whatever."

"Oh yeah____" I said. "And just what kind of energy___?" He smiled and winked.

"No don't worry. I didn't slip you an aphrodisiac." he whispered.

"Let me see your palms, Shay. Ah hah."

"What?"

"Nothing?"

"Murphy, what are you doing?"

"Reading your palms. Shhhhh. Hmmmm___.

"What do you see? You saw something in my palms.

Tell me. Please, Murphy___"

But he wouldn't. He laid on a large pillow and appeared to be studying the ceiling for a second. Then he said mysteriously, "The light should always be your own."

He told me about some of the people he had met along the way. We also talked about the disturbance that had taken place at Yodel's and discovered that even though it was tragic, it contained so much humor that we found ourselves laughing hysterically.

"And that's exactly why I talk to our young brothers," Murphy explained. "Brother Creighton is a good example of what black people with self-hatred are capable of doing and you know what I want you to do? Stop calling him crazy. He's a victim."

"Yeah, he is. I feel bad for him," I admitted. I thought about Creighton for a few moments. I had practically known him all my life. Lester Creighton was his name. He'd been negative from the time he was a child. His existence seemed almost fruitless, but Murphy said that Creighton's actions that evening had a deep purpose, which was mainly to affirm to the black people there the necessity of having pride in themselves.

"I'm gonna pay him a visit," Murphy blurted. "That brother needs to know that black people are not his enemy."

Sprawled upon his pillow, chewing on what resembled a twig, Murphy studied me closely.

"Murphy, why are you staring at me like that?"

"I like your humility, baby. People have got to remember to stay humble, cause you see, it was the tiny ant that taught man how to build great civilizations."

Together, we read his book of poems. No one could deny that they were true masterpieces, so stirring, yet written with such simplicity.

"Know the difference between a wannabe writer and a true writer, Shay?"

"No. What is it?" I asked eagerly.

"A wannabe's words flow from the mind but a true writer's words flow from the heart. It's all about sincerity and passion. The heart always wins. And when are you going to stop calling me Murphy? Try my new name. It's not that hard. N-to-mo..."

We laughed as I tried to pronounce his new name. It took many tries to get it right and I am ashamed to admit today that I have forgotten it.

Murphy performed many miracles for me in the room that day. Hand in hand we walked his sea. Words of truth and wisdom flowed so sweetly from his throat that I, insatiable, drank them like wine. Then drunken with truth I entered inside his temple and he fed me five thousand times. It was then that I discovered that Murphy was not of this world. It was imperative that he should keep his heaven, for gods have nowhere else to go.

We made love again, more ardently. Afterwards he lay upon his back, gloriously naked. I laid my face across his chest and allowed my eyes to roam down his long lean body. When my eyes settled upon his feet, to my amazement, *Murphy had grown back his toe!* Two weeks later the light had traveled on.

I was never the same after spending time with Murphy. That spring I experienced unfamiliar and wondrous things. Afloat the dirty smog I was able to spot silver lined clouds. I understood that early morning foghorns did not disturb the silence, but were actually hallowed cries that beckoned one to listen to his own soul that often calls out in lone silence. I realized that Creighton was really an unfortunate by-product of black nihilism. Ella, I learned, had been truly helpless in the arms of her pimp, who like Murphy, was dangerously charismatic and addictive. Yet, the man laced her soul with her unfortunate environment then clipped her wings. Her greatest mistake was not the whore she had once been but the fact that she had failed to value her own light. Old Man Payne, I learned, was wrong for sending the high school girls running from his limp useless penis, yet, his perversion did not exclude a deep mourning for and celebration of youth.

A few years later, I searched for Murphy in dreadlocked men, but found only lousy Bob Marley imitations and men who were just themselves, regular, not a Murphy. Reluctantly, I went down my own path and became an art instructor at a neighborhood community center, and a soldier for the local 'struggle.' I had a child, but I did not want a mere mortal man for a husband so I have been divorced for years.

I didn't see Murphy again until years later when he came home for his aunt's funeral. He proved his authenticity, for he did not return as a retired pimp might, wearing long fingernails and a cowboy hat. In fact, he had become a fairly well known activist, still tackling 'bad mouthed life', daring it to push a warrior around. He had a full salt and peppered beard and his antennas had grayed at the temples and nearly touched the back of his knees. He was also wearing thick eyeglasses. His sight had undoubtedly grown quite poor from the enormous amount of reading he'd done. We left the gathering of friends and relatives on the porch and took a long walk hand in hand.

"I never got married," Murphy started. "I had relationships with a few activists sisters along the way but you were the only one who could touch my light. And man, I was really scared about that. I was afraid that you could turn me into a family man and then Jah's purpose for blowing life into my nostrils would not have been fulfilled. To be honest though, it might have been an easier path if I had been a family man." He smiled nervously.

"I read how you organized the black college students in Florida." I said with an admiration that was very obvious.

"Yeah, that was a job but somebody had to enlighten them. Every campus administrator in that state was on my back but we need our educated young folks to be on our side. Our people are regressing fast. And most of the students didn't get my message. Ain't that something? I risk going to jail and half of them didn't even hear me." He sighed heavily.

"Murphy, they heard. It's just that time has changed our people. They're forgetting we came here in chains. We have to keep reminding them that we only have the illusion of being free."

"I hope it's not too late. More than half of our people don't have a clue that there is a war going on in this country and they're in it. And ain't no God coming out of the sky to fight our battles for us. I'm sorry but we need to wake up! Jah gave us good brains but we waste them on fantasy. Listen, it's been hundreds of years now and we're still looking up in the sky for help. If we haven't learned by now that Jah wants us to help ourselves then shame on us. And I won't lie, I pray too, but I do it to fill up with Jah's higher power. You pray, Shay?"

"I uh, no Murphy. Not anymore. I do meditate."

"Well, that's prayer too. That's what it's about. Jah is inside. A lot of our people think he's somewhere out there separate from them. And our Christian brothers and sisters better hope they get it together cause if Jesus does come he's gonna be mad as hell for us letting religion and beliefs stop us from coming together to fight evil. Jah gave us strength and wisdom to change our reality and make heaven right here on earth." He pulled me closer to his side and said, "Let's go up this street. Can you believe that's the rec center?" Murphy stood staring at the recreation center and was probably thinking of how he used to lecture a group of mannish boys in black history. He took my hand and we walked on.

"There's just so much I've wanted to explain to you," Murphy continued. "I called myself a fool over and over for leaving you and I started to send for you but I found out you had a son and the way I lived was no life for a lady and child. I slept on dirt floors half the time, went hungry a lot. But still, after all these years, no other woman has been able to take your place."

He stopped walking abruptly and lifted my chin to his. I saw that same something in his eyes that had always looked right through me and I tried to turn away but he wouldn't let me.

"No, don't look away," he said. "Again, after all these years, no other woman has been able to take your place."

I assured Murphy that I felt the same way. No other man could ever take his place. So we agreed right then and there that we would come together again; our missions having been met in the mixed up mangled lives of our people and love one another again.

Murphy spent the next few days at my home and nothing had ever been so wonderful as waking up to the only man I have ever loved. One morning he rose, kissed me several times and packed his bags. Again the *light* traveled on.

I thought I had understood life enough to part with him joyfully but as time moved on my world grew saddened, deep and troubled. I yearned for the only love I had known. Sparks of happiness came only whenever he would phone, which was not often. If only he had been a loser, a lousy lover or perhaps a pretentious brother, then I could have gotten along very well without him but I dragged around as little pieces of my spirit drifted away.

One Friday evening after I had overindulged in a bottle of Chardonnay at a downtown club, Murphy *stepped out of me*. He took a seat across the table and just stared into my eyes. I swallowed my emptiness with two shots of gin and clung to a false courage that bade me to confront a denial of truth. I had placed myself in bondage for years after Murphy had led me to freedom. I had not moved on after being loved by Murphy because I had not worked on my own light. Murphy shook his head, rose from the table, kissed my mind and headed for the door. He took with him his stolen light that had kept me afloat and jerked the hem of his garment from between my frantic fingertips. Suddenly my feet began to sink and I found myself drowning and the watchtower had been shut down. I choked on the waters as I was tossed and buried in the waves, then miraculously I began to swim. I heard myself muttering and cursing life softly as my tears made tiny puddles on the table. It was not unlike the kind of crying my Great Uncle James had done whenever he had drunk corn liquor. I had realized that it was lonely walking the sea to the light of my own watchtower. I had begun to miss Murphy terribly.

"You alright, Ma'am? Ma'am, are you okay?" A concerned young lady asked me.

I tried to speak, but words would not come from my trembling lips.

"Forget her," the young lady's friend said. "She's drunk."

"What? Drunk? Excuse me!" I said vehemently. *"But I have been loved by Murphy!"*

The two young ladies stood with blank faces. They did not understand. How could they? They knew nothing about the way Murphy's tongue had licked away my tears or how his lips had formed the words, "BABY GIRL" and had made my toes curl up.

Sometimes I allow other men to occupy the void in my life but they do not fill it up. It is just so. They accept without question that there is a well of hunger within me that runs deep but it is not for them. They accept that there is a distant soul in me that they will never know and touch. Most do not even bother. They sit at my feet and make useless chatter as I watch the calendar, my evolving gray hairs and signs in the sky for Murphy's return. Like a blind fool in a dark alley, I stumble through life, fumbling with my own lantern and longing for that sacrificial light that saved and slaughtered me simultaneously. Still? Ah, so be it. True love will never die. You can't poison it or rationalize it away and if you manage to put it asleep, like Lazarus it rises again and again.

Once, my brother told me that no one on earth did *not* lie.

"Murphy ain't never lied," I told him.

"Well, then he must be a god or something," he said flatly.

I left it at that.

Today I burn a light at the side door for the man that will return to lay his weary head upon my lap. It is the strangest thing...sometimes I think I believe in god again, but then Murphy comes to mind. I do not think that it is Murphy's Jah, or Allah, Buddha, or any other familiar god that has given Murphy life. Perhaps there are gods, and then there are other *Gods*. But I believe that Murphy emerged on his own accord and he is the God above his head. Yet, in the event that I am wrong, and some God has managed to blow perfect life into Murphy's nostrils, then the question I ask of the universe is this: How can I get under the same *God* as he?

THE END

It's my journey, taint none of yourn's. Might not be the best cause surely there's the holes in the soles and bunions and the aching knees and I can't forget the bulging disks and bill collectors and eviction notices. But my journey don' made me me and I got a right to the little piece of forest I walk upon. Be it a struggle, you jest know, the nature of these twists and turns don' made me beautiful and stand out like a field of morning glories on a zigzagged hillside.

Thank you for purchasing this Natroy Publishing product.
If you have enjoyed this book, we would love for you
to recommend it to others. There will also be many
more titles to choose from as new works are being
released quite frequently.
We publish children's, teens and adults literature.
We also publish theatrical plays, poetry, CD's and are
moving into DVD's.

Please visit our website: www.natroypublishing.com
for more information about our literary collection.
If you have enjoyed this book feel free to e-mail us an
encouraging remark. (See the e-mail address below.)

We offer exciting, book signings by our authors that include
storytelling, music, workshops and skits. Consider
scheduling one at your site and give your attendees
something a little different than a traditional book
signing.

If you are interested, please contact us:
natroypub@gmail.com

Always thinking about the next project...

Ife-Gail F. Young, holds a B.A. in Dramatic Arts. We find no need to give her unending praises and accolades because her numerous bold and refreshing works speaks for themselves. She has produced superb thought-provoking, controversial and uplifting writings with the imagery and power to enchant her readers.

In addition to being a novelist she is a prolific playwright. Her works have appeared on stages in several states, including New York. She has won creative writing awards and is also a vocalist, actress, storyteller, lightweight guitarist & illustrator.

She is available for readings, performances and book signings

ATTN: LIBRARIES, SCHOOLS, CHURCHES All
AGENCIES AND/OR ORGANIZATIONS

To schedule a reading, book signing or storytelling
performance, send an
e-mail to:

natroypub@gmail.com

Give Your Child A Healthy Reading Experience...
'BINA AND THE BEANPOLE'
FAST GROWING IN POPULARITY
A MUST HAVE FOR AFRICAN-AMERICAN CHILDREN

What Is This Book About?

It is a children's series, Chapter Books with a purpose to
inform, empower, heal, and inspire African American youth
to greatness by helping steer them away from unhealthy
values and negative behaviors that are damaging and
nonproductive. Told from a 12 year old girl's perspective,
the readers grow to love the main character, her siblings
and family. This Coming of Age series promotes Literacy,
African/African-American History, and Promotes Family
and Community.

Visit: www.binaandthebeanpole.com
for more information.

YOU CAN PURCHASE
OTHER WORKS BY THIS AUTHOR AT:
www.amazon.com

*Search For The Author's Name: Ife-Gail Young
Or Search By Book Title.*

<u>*Coming Soon*</u>:
'Journey Through A Zigzagged Forest,' Vol. 2 –

"After All Is Said And Done" – This novel looks at society's values with scutinizing microscopes.